WHATNOT
TAKES
CHARGE

LINDA NEWBERY
GEORGIE RIPPER

For Olivia Hope Burningham
L.N.
For Dad with love
G.R.

EGMONT
We bring stories to life

Book Band: White

First published in Great Britain 2006
by Egmont UK Ltd
239 Kensington High Street, London W8 6SA
Text copyright © Linda Newbery 2006
Illustrations copyright © Georgie Ripper 2006
The author and illustrator have asserted their moral rights
ISBN 978 1 4052 1205 2
10 9 8 7 6 5 4 3 2 1
A CIP catalogue record for this title is available from the British Library.
Printed in Singapore
42525/4

EGMONT LUCKY COIN

Our story began over a century ago, when seventeen-year-old Egmont Harald Petersen found a coin in the street.

He was on his way to buy a flyswatter, a small hand-operated printing machine that he then set up in his tiny apartment.

The coin brought him such good luck that today Egmont has offices in over 30 countries around the world. And that lucky coin is still kept at the company's head offices in Denmark.

Contents

Red Bananas

A DOG OF MANY TALENTS

Whatnot was Tim's dog, and the best dog in the world. But only Tim and his family knew just how special Whatnot was.

Whatnot came from a family of rather famous dogs. They had skills. They had talents. They often had their photos in the local paper, for winning prizes and trophies. Whatnot's brother, Westmoreland William the Bold, had won a place in the final of a competition

Westmore Wins again

in London.

Whatnot had never won a prize – but then Whatnot had never entered for a competition.

When the posters went up for the school fete, Tim saw

Dog scoops top prize

Whatnot's big chance. There would be stalls, competitions, a bouncy castle, a tea tent and a Fancy Dress Relay for parents and helpers.

Top Dog!

5

Most exciting of all, there would be a competition for dogs.

'Whatnot can do that!' Tim told Ajay, pointing to OBEDIENCE AND AGILITY COMPETITION. OPEN TO ALL DOGS AND THEIR HANDLERS.

'Whatnot?' huffed Ajay. 'Obedient? He wasn't obedient when he stole my cricket ball. Or when he hid in the bushes and wouldn't come out. Or when he tangled me up in his lead.'

'He can learn,' said Tim. 'Whatnot's a dog of many talents, Grandad says.'

Ajay looked at the poster. 'He'd better learn fast. You've got two weeks.'

DISOBEDIENCE CLASS

Lots of helpers were needed for the fête.
Grandad put his name down to make cakes.

'I'll have a Grand Baking Day,' he said,
rubbing his hands.

Tim liked Grandad's Baking Days. So did
Whatnot.

Mum and three of her friends were going in
for the Fancy Dress Relay, dressed as pirates.

Mum planned her costume. She ran laps in the park.

She customised her trainers to look piratical.

Louisa and Flora were going to help Flora's mum with the face-painting.

Ajay was working on something for the Art competition, in secret.

Tim was busy with Whatnot. On Monday evening, he and Grandad took Whatnot to his first Obedience Class. Whatnot loved it. All those dogs! All those smiley mouths and waggy tails! He was so excited that he couldn't help dashing in mad circles when he was supposed to be Walking at Heel.

'He'll learn,' said Grandad.

'He's a bad influence!' said a man with a perfectly-behaved beagle called Brodie.

'Give him time,' said Mrs McLeish, the trainer.

How much time? Tim thought. The competition was on Saturday week.

'Sit!' he tried. 'Stay!' Whatnot could never Sit and Stay without wriggling and whimpering, but he was doing his best – until a gust of wind made the door slam.

11

ccCCRRRRRR-WHUMMMPPP!

Whatnot was off! Dragging Tim, he charged into the cupboard-space under the stage, and cringed there, quivering. Tim had to coax him out with chocolate buttons.

'That dog,' sniffed Brodie's owner, 'seems to think this is Disobedience Class!'

'He's always been frightened of loud noises,' Tim explained. 'It's not his fault.'

'He's a bit excitable!' said Mrs McLeish.

'He'll learn,' said Grandad. 'Give him time.'

GRAND BAKING DAY

The day before the fête, Grandad put on an
apron and took over the kitchen. He was
never happier than when making cakes. And
today he was making *hundreds* of cakes.
Chocolate cakes, carrot cakes, fairy cakes and
lemon cakes. Flapjacks, brandysnaps, muffins
and tiffin.

Whatnot sat under the table, twitching his
nose at all the delicious smells. Candied peel
and coconut. Almonds and
apricots. Marzipan and
maple syrup, pecans and
peanuts and peppermint.
It was enough to make
a dog drool.

Whatnot went to the park with Tim, to
practise being Obedient.

'Now listen, Whatnot,' Tim told him sternly.
'This is serious. You've got to do your best
tomorrow. OK?'

No wriggling!

Whatnot whuffed. He knew something
important was going to happen, and he
really wanted to do his best.

So, even though a grey
squirrel skittered down a tree
trunk, and two ducks
sidled up from the lake, and
a plump cat strutted along by
the fence, he only looked
at them sideways.

He kept his attention
on Tim.

18

Fetch!

That was harder.

It was much more fun to run off with the ball than to bring it back to Tim.

Much more fun to make Tim grovel in the bushes or reach under the roundabout.

19

But he was on Best Behaviour, so he did
what he was supposed to do.

Tim gave him a big pat and hug when the
practice was over. 'Good boy, Whatnot! Do as
well as that tomorrow, and we'll get first
prize, I bet!'

Good
boy!

Whatever was happening tomorrow, it
wasn't going to be much of a challenge for a
dog like Whatnot.

WHATNOT'S TURN

The school field was full of tents and stalls, a Bouncy Castle and an ice-cream van.

The grass had been mown and the running-track marked out with white paint. There was wellie-whanging. There were skittles.

There was a special ring roped off for the dog show, and there were lots and lots of dogs, waiting for the competition.

Huge dogs. Tiny dogs. Shaggy dogs. Fierce dogs.

There was a judge, looking stern.

And there was Whatnot, rather nervous.

'You'll be all right, Whatnot!' Tim whispered. 'Just remember what we've practised.'

Whatnot whuffed, but he had only one ear cocked towards Tim. The other was pointing at a cross-looking bull terrier.

You can do it, Whatnot!

Grandad unloaded boxes and tins full of cakes and buns, and went into the tea tent.

SCHOOL FÊTE

Louisa went off to start painting faces.

Aha, me hearties!

Mum adjusted her eye-patch and went to find the other pirates.

Tim and Whatnot stood by the ring-ropes. First in the competition was Brodie, from the Obedience Class, doing everything perfectly. He sat and stayed, he jumped the hurdles, he wove between skittles, he fetched a ball and presented it to his owner.

'That's how you do it, Whatnot!' Tim said.

He's good!

Next came a
brown-and-white
spaniel, rather fat
and slow. He
knocked down two jumps.
Then it was Whatnot's turn.
'Good luck!' shouted Mum. She had come
over to watch, but just at that moment a
voice over the loudspeaker called for the
runners in the Fancy Dress Relay.

Go, Whatnot!

Tim, with Whatnot trotting at heel, jogged
into the ring. The steward blew his whistle.
Off they went, towards the first hurdles.
Whatnot hurtled over them, barking happily.
He could do this!

'Here, boy!' Tim called, running
towards the skittles. Whatnot knew he
had to weave through them. He'd just
started, careful not to knock one over, when:

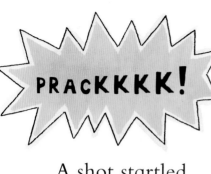

PRACKKKK!

A shot startled everyone – the steward for the Fancy Dress Relay was using a real, old-fashioned starting pistol!

First I'll beat you, then I'll eat you!

The noise hurt Whatnot's ears. Before he knew what he was doing, he'd scattered the skittles and streaked right out of the ring.

'Whatnot! Come back!' yelled Tim.

JOB DONE

Whatnot was too frightened to hear. His ears
were pressed flat back. He ran as
fast as he could – then saw
the Fancy Dress
runners.

Watch out!

Pirates and chickens and milkmaids and
Draculas, clutching their cloaks or their hats
or their heads, were scampering along.

A memory stirred in Whatnot's mind.

His father had been a champion sheepdog, and had told him stories about it. As a pup, Whatnot had thought that one day *he* might be a sheepdog.

In his panic and confusion, he saw running legs and flying feet. Here was his chance!

Clearly, it was his job to round up all these scurrying creatures. There would be a pen somewhere near, waiting for him to herd them into it. He'd known something special was happening today, and this must be it!

He dashed over to the first runners and darted at their heels.

A teddy-bear turned round in alarm. 'Hey, what–'

Whoah!

Count Dracula veered across the track.

A chicken almost lost its head.

34

Whatnot ran round the outside, nudging, whuffing. He was getting the idea of this!

Where was he herding them, though? Then he saw the entrance to the tea tent, where Grandad stood waving his arms. There was lots of space inside – that must be the pen!

Over here, Whatnot!

The runners were making bleating noises, just like sheep.

'Hey, what?'

'Flipping heck!'

'Call him off, someone!'

'WHATNOT!'

That was Mum – running skew-whiff because of her eye-patch. Whatnot felt encouraged. He was doing rather well at this – why had he never tried it before?

He gathered up lots more people from the side of the track, until he had a good-sized flock.

He kept them neatly together, sprinting round to one side and then the other, always watching. He never actually nipped anyone's heels, but he looked as if he might, so everyone took care to keep just ahead of him. As more and more people came over to see what was happening, Whatnot guided them towards the tea tent.

A clown decided that the tent was the
safest place to be, and waddled inside.
All the others followed. Whatnot
was delighted. Easy! He lay
down by the entrance,
panting with pride.

SCHOOL FÊ

Let's go
in here.

Job done!

WHATNOT IN HIDING

'Whatnot! Whatnot!' Tim was panting for breath, his face scarlet with embarrassment. 'What have you done?'

Sorry!

The tent was now so full that there was hardly room for another person inside. 'I'm really sorry,' Tim said to a chef in a tall hat. 'He didn't mean it. He's scared of loud noises–' But no one was listening to him.

Everyone was looking at Grandad's cakes, pushing closer to the tables for a better look.

'Hey! They look good,' said a cowboy.

'Chocolate brownies – my favourite!' said a ballet dancer.

'Got any money?' asked a fireman.

'Cinnamon buns – yum!' said a bride.

Grandad and the other helpers squeezed themselves round behind the tables, and started selling cakes as fast as they could.

Tim and Whatnot slunk away.

WHATNOT THE WINNER

Tim felt so ashamed that
he didn't want to show his face
– or Whatnot's. He
and Whatnot hid in
the trees behind the
infants' playground.

Whatnot was
feeling very pleased
with himself. He'd
never had such fun!

Sigh.

'You did your best,
Whatnot,' Tim told him sadly. 'It wasn't your
fault the pistol went off.'

Whatnot had ruined the whole fête! The races
seemed to have stopped – nearly everyone was
in the tea tent, though there were a few people
and dogs over by the Dog Ring.

Tim sat gloomily on a swing,
and didn't even cheer up
when Whatnot licked
his nose.

They sat there for a very long time – until
Grandad walked past the trees,
looking for them.

'Grandad!' Tim
called.

Grandad came over.
'Well! Good old Whatnot!
That was brilliant, wasn't it?'

'Uh?' said Tim.

'All that's left is crumbs,'
Grandad told him. 'We've taken pots of money!

There you are!

The Relay Race had to be postponed – the runners are too full of cake! So it's going to happen last thing, when they've had time to recover. Everyone says it's the best fête ever! Come on – I saved you a fudge brownie, your favourite. You can give Whatnot a piece.'

Great!

Tim was sure that everyone would be cross with him and Whatnot. Instead, as they walked across the field, people clapped and pointed and cheered.

Ajay ran up. 'Hey! Come and look at this!' He was so excited that he did a little dance.

'What?'

Tim, Grandad and Whatnot followed him to the Arts and Plants tent.

On the way, they passed the winner of the Dog Obedience competition – Brodie, wearing his rosette and looking as smug as his owner.

Ajay led the way to the farthest table,
which was marked ART COMPETITION.

'How about this?'

FIRST PRIZE, said a certificate.
AJAY KAPOOR. And his picture was
wearing a big blue rosette.

'Hey!' said Grandad. 'So Whatnot's a winner after all! Well done, both of you!'

'Brilliant!' Tim slapped Ajay on the back. Ajay beamed with pride, and fixed the rosette to Whatnot's collar.

You're a winner, Whatnot!

Well done, Ajay!

Whatnot sat thumping his tail, looking up at the picture.

It had been a brilliant afternoon, and now he had a rosette to wear! And he was sure he'd heard Grandad say FUDGE BROWNIE.

Woof!